MW01519611

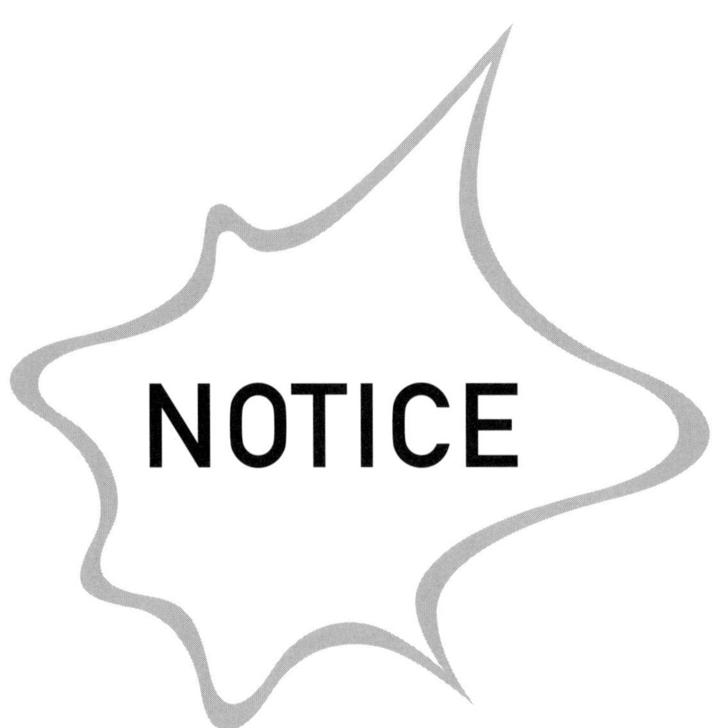
NOTICE

GEOFFREY

BROWN

Gutter Press

The publisher gratefully acknowledges the assistance of The Ontario Arts Council and The Canada Council for the Arts.

Canadian Cataloguing in Publication Data
Geoffrey Brown, 1965-
Notice
A Ken Sparling Book
ISBN 1-896356-22-2
I. Title.
PS8553.R68497N67 1998 C813'.54 C98-933037-0
PR9199.3.B6978N67 1998

Published by Gutter Press, P.O. Box 600, Station Q,
Toronto, Ontario, Canada M4T 2N4
voice: (416) 822.8708, fax: (416) 822.8709
email: gutter@gutterpress.com

Represented and Distributed in Canada by
Publishers Group West Canada, 250A Carlton St.
Toronto, Ontario, Canada M5L 2L1
Toll Free: 1-800 747.8147 fax: (416) 934.1410
Distributed in the U.S. and abroad by D.A.P.
Distributed Art Publishers, Inc.
155 Sixth Avenue, 2nd Floor,
New York, NY 10013-1507
To order, call 1-800 338.BOOK

Design...4dt (4 designerly types)
Manufactured in Canada

Portions of this work were originally published, in somewhat different form, in *Blood & Aphorisms*, *Broken Pencil* and *The New Quarterly*. My thanks to Penny Cousineau and Ken Sparling.

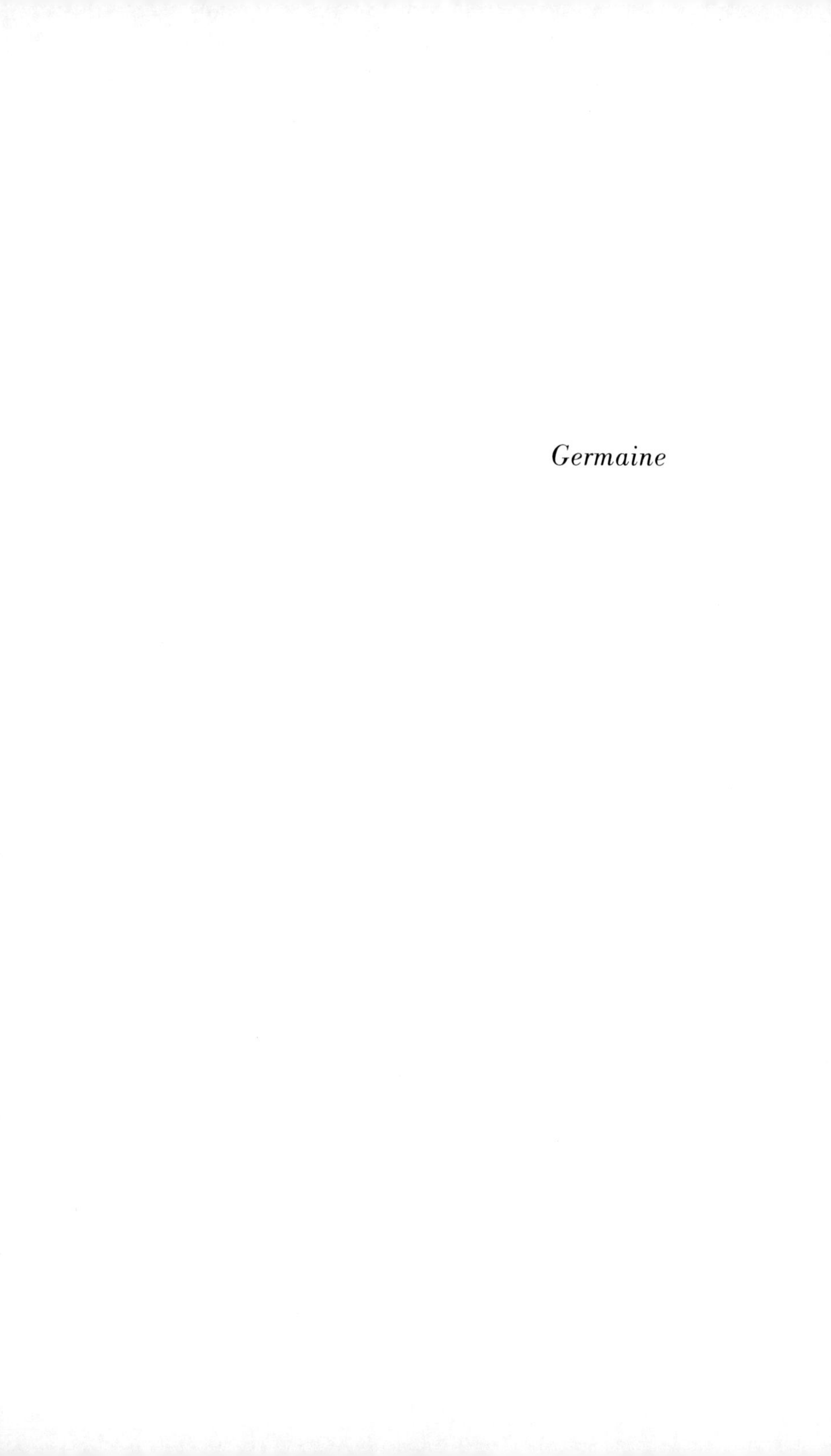

Germaine

They took me. They came and got me out of bed and took me. They told me not to move. "Wait here until further notice," they said.

He cut it up. He cut it up and then he cut the pieces of it up and then he cut them up again. He kept on cutting them up. He couldn't stop. He just kept cutting. There were pieces of it everywhere. Little pieces. In the sink and on the floor. Little tiny pieces. He kept cutting them and cutting them and they were everywhere. He stopped and looked. My God! he thought. He put the cutter down and got a broom and started sweeping. He used his hands and swept the sink, the floor. He swept it into little piles and then he made a bigger pile. He got a garbage bag and put it down beside the pile. He put the pile inside the bag. He used his hands to pick it up. He tied the bag and went outside. He went outside and put the bag down by the curb. There were other bags beside the curb. His hands felt wet. He held up his hands and looked at them and then he wiped them on his legs. He looked at them again.

I got up. I wanted to go home. I closed my eyes. Took deep breaths. I clenched my teeth. My hands made fists. I sat back down.

We were out of milk. But we were always out of milk. Or we were always running out of milk. Or if not milk then something else. Eggs or bread or cheese.

I spent a long time looking at them. I wanted to make sure that I had seen them. I wanted to make sure that if I came across them again somewhere, I would know them.

We got in and went. I was in the back. I liked it in the back. It was better in the back. I kept quiet while he drove. I knew he liked it quiet. He had told me once before. He had yelled it once before. He held the door as I got out. I made sure the door was locked. He took my hand and walked with me. I was looking down. I was not afraid.

He tried to think of something. He tried to think of something quick.

Okay. I'll try again. I've tried already. I'll try again. This time, I'll try harder.

I said, "Come here."

I said, "Come over here."

I said, "Come on, come here, come over here."

I had my hand behind my back. There was nothing in it.

I tore them in two. *I tore them in two*, I thought. I had torn them in two. I tore them in two again.

He bent down and looked. He could see them clearly. He knew who they were. He knew what they were doing.

There was something there. I could hear it. I went over with a flashlight. I stood still and listened. I could not see anything. I turned the flashlight off. Waited. Nothing. Maybe it was gone. Maybe they were gone.

I used to drink tea. I used to drink it every evening, after dinner, after I had all the dishes done. Now I drink tomato juice.

It rains here a lot.
  It is snowing now.

I exercise. I do push-ups. Sit-ups. I do them everyday. I do sit-ups everyday. I don't do push-ups everyday. But I do sit-ups everyday. Some days I don't do anything.

He cut it into pieces. Cut it into pieces, they told him. Now they wanted it together. They wanted it put back. They wanted him to put it back together.

I counted them. I felt foolish, but I counted them. I forget how many I had. There were quite a few. More than before.

I could hear it start. I could hear it start and I could hear it stop. I went to the window. There was nothing there.

Dinner was done. The dishes were done. I was drying my hands. My wife was running a bath.

I tried to stay quiet. I knew they couldn't see me. They might hear me, though, I thought. So I stayed quiet. Held my breath. I did not move.

He put in one and then another one. He had two stuck in already so he doubled it. He pushed them in and waited. There was no response. He held them there and got another. Put that one in as well. He pushed the others up. He held them there. There was no response. He had put them in. All of them were in. They were all pushed in.

There was nothing there. I went out to look. I had heard something, I thought. I thought that I had heard something. But there was nothing there. I went back inside.

I wish I hadn't started. I wish I'd never even thought. I'll do it, though. I will do it.

He got up and went out after him.
"Where are you going?"
He was in the street.
"Come back."

I decided not to use it. I tried to use it. I couldn't use it. Now I have another. It is not much better. It doesn't feel right. I might get the old one back. I might try to get the old one back.

I knocked it over. I knocked it over and it broke. It was not an accident. I wanted it to break. I wanted it to shatter. So I pretended not to see it. I moved my arm over. I heard it fall. I heard it break.

It did not arrive. I was told that it was coming, that it was on its way, but it did not arrive. Not today, at any rate. It may come tomorrow. Or later on this week.

It was taking him a long time. It was taking him longer than he thought. He was doing it fast, but it was taking him too long. He didn't have much time. They would be coming soon. If he didn't get through it soon, they would be coming.

I may go today. I wasn't going to go today. I was going to wait and go another day. But I don't know. I may go today.

The telephone rings and I don't answer it. It rings again.

My wife yells.

"Are you going to answer?"

I let it ring once more.

I did everything that I was told. I put everything precisely where I was supposed to put it. There was nothing out of place. Nothing did not fit. This is not remarkable. This in itself is not remarkable. I know. It has all been done before. But has it ever been done better? Has anybody ever done it better?

It bothers me. I shouldn't let it bother me, but it bothers me. I don't know why. I don't think it's fair. I will not deny it. I don't think it's fair. I should just ignore it.

He hit the ball hard and watched it go. I watched it, too. We both watched it. It landed on the road and rolled. I went over.

Throw it here! my brother yelled.

I bent down and picked it up. The ball was in the ditch. There was water in the ditch. The ball was in the water. I picked up the ball and wiped it off. I held it in my hand and rubbed it.

My brother yelled.

I went back across the road and threw it. I threw it hard.

This one's not as good. I mean, this one's not as good as the other one. They're supposed to be the same. I was told they were the same. But clearly they are not. This one's not as good. It doesn't feel as good.

He was there, but hidden, hiding. I said something to him anyway. I knew he could hear me.

I pulled it apart. It was in pieces on the floor. I was supposed to be fixing it. I was the one who said I could fix it. But I couldn't fix it. I was just talking. That was just talking. I didn't think they would really believe me. I didn't think they would say, Okay, fix it. But I don't care. So what? Who cares?

I didn't do it. I could have done it. I didn't. But I could have. I could have done it easily. I had every opportunity to do it. Which is why I'm not surprised to find out now that someone else has done it. It was bound to happen. It had to happen. At some point, by some means, it had to happen. Not that it makes any difference now. But still. It would have been no trouble. It would have been no trouble at all.

He would open it, then close it. He kept opening it and closing it. I wanted him to stop. Stop, I told him.

It was out and in his hand. He was pulling on it. He was pulling on it and she was watching. He pulled and she watched. He showed her. He was showing her how she should do it. He held it out and pulled on it. "See," he said. She looked. She made a fist and squeezed.

He parted it and put it in. He used his hands to guide it in. But it would not go all the way. He couldn't get it all the way. He pulled it out and tried again. He parted it, guided it. It went farther this time. He bent down and looked at it. He decided that was far enough.

She wasn't looking at him. He said something, and she answered, but she wasn't looking at him.

Look at me, he said.

It didn't matter much, though, really. He would look at her. He liked to look at her. She was something he could look at.

They were staring down. The two of them. They stood there, staring down.

"Is it dead?" one said.

The other one kicked it.

"It seems to be."

"I'll count to three," one said. He counted.

They picked it up. They brought it to the car, put it in the trunk. They left the keys in the ignition.

He pulled it apart. He did it with his hands. Inside it was pink. He put in a finger. He put in another. It felt like something he had felt before. He could not remember what. He moved his fingers. He moved his fingers. He tried to put in a third finger. The first two fell out. He pulled it apart again.

She kept quiet. She found out about it in the morning, but she didn't say anything. She didn't say anything all day. She must have found it difficult. I would have found it difficult. We were in the kitchen. We were finished dinner. I was doing dishes. Outside it was snowing. I knew what was coming. I knew what had happened. I heard her start to cry.

I am going to keep on doing it. Doing it or doing them. Whatever.

What am I supposed to do with these? I mean, what am I supposed to do?

He wasn't going to do it. He was not. "I'm not going to do it," he said.

"You have to do it," they told him. "You have to try."

So he tried.

He tried to do it.

"You have to try," they said.

He tried again.

This time she was cutting him.

"Tell me when it hurts," she said.

"It hurts," he said.

She kept cutting.

"Tell me when."

They spent the morning digging. The hole was deep enough by noon, but they went on and dug some more. They wanted to do it right this time. By dusk they were done. They stood back and looked at it. They looked at one another. It was there. There was a bulge. It was small, but it was there. It would flatten out in time, they thought. All it needed was a little time.

He was going to do it. He had said he would and he was going to. For a price he would do anything, he decided. He would do this for a price. He would do it first and get paid later, he decided. He knew he'd get paid. He felt confident. He thought he should do it while he had the confidence. He had it now and he would do it now.

I guess they were glad. You've got to figure they were glad. At least, back then, at that time. I know myself, I would have been glad.

They didn't give me a number. A reservation number. They didn't give me one. Are they not supposed to give me a reservation number? They used to give you one. I know they used to give you one. Maybe I should call them back.

It will be dismissed. I think it will be dismissed. They won't know what to make of it. They'll say there's nothing there. They'll say there's not enough.

It would not go in. He could not believe it. He was on his knees beside the bed and he could not believe it. Never in his life before had anything like this occurred. He tried turning it around. He turned it upside down. But it would not go in. No matter what he did, it still would not go in. He could not believe it.

In the end it did go in.

In any case, he got it in.

It would not go in and then it did go in. It was easy, really. He was on his knees, beside the bed.

He asked her would she do it and she told him she would not. She said that it was not something that she would do. She told him she'd do anything for him, but not that. She once told him there was nothing she would not be glad to do for him. She meant it, too. She would do anything for him. Anything but that.

I went on over. He was already out. He had cut off quite a bit. There were pieces of it. They looked small. I had brought the bags. I had smaller bags and bigger bags. He said to start off with the smaller bags. I could put the smaller bags inside the bigger bags. I watched him cutting. He cut one off and held it up. He handed it to me. I pulled out a bag.

I want to use the same word over and over. I want to use it over and over and over again. So that the whole thing is just one word.

I let it get away. I shouldn't say I let it. I didn't let it get away. I did not let it get away. All the same, it did. It got away. It was up to me to stop it. I was supposed to stop it. But I didn't. I didn't stop it. I didn't even try.

Everyone is leaving. Everyone is quitting or going away or leaving. Watch them. Watch them leave and not look back.

I'm not going to keep all this. When I am done, I mean. I'm not going to keep it. I will throw it out. Or something. I don't know. I don't want to know.

I took it. I pretended it was mine. I held it up. I put it in my pocket. I walked away.

He said we should go someplace where we would not be seen. I followed him. We did what we had said we would. We made sure that no one saw us. We made sure they never did.

It was in my hand. I was going to take it. I was getting ready to. Then I thought I might get caught. "This time I'll get caught," I thought.

I knew what would happen. I had not been told, but I knew. I knew where and when and I was ready.

I wasn't going to touch it. Honestly, I wasn't. For several days I didn't. Not at all. Not even once. Then I did.

I search systematically. I go from room to room, from floor to floor. I look through cupboards and in closets. I search the basement, barn, the attic. There is no place I don't look. But I do not find anything. So I go back, begin again.

We took turns. First I hit him, then he hit him. We used a stick. We hit him hard. We hit him on his back and on his legs. We were not afraid. Once we hit him on the face. We promised we would stop. But we were boys and we were bad.

When he first approached me I had no idea who he was. He introduced himself and I remembered. I took his hand. His face bore similarities. I let him buy me lunch. He did all the talking. I didn't ask how he had found me. I let him talk. Then I left. I told him not to follow. I kept looking back. I still look back.

I didn't know what it was. There it was in front of me, but I had no idea what it was. It had arms, it had legs. It even had a penis. Or what looked to me to be a penis. But it was not a boy. It was not a man. It was nothing I had ever seen before. It ran away the moment it saw me. It turned around and ran away. I didn't try to follow. I was glad that it was gone.

I wasn't going to keep it. I wasn't sure I should. But I did not know what to do. I couldn't give it back. Too much time had passed. And I was not about to throw it out. I could not consider that. So I did what I could. I did the only thing I could.

I was not supposed to look. I knew it, too. I knew that I was not supposed to look. That was something I just knew. Not that I was ever told. I was never told. No one ever told me. No one ever said, Don't look. My father never did. My father never said, Don't look Geoff. Don't ever look.

I watch from the window. The man approaches slowly. He's holding something in his hand. I don't know what. It could be a book. Or it might be a box. It could be anything. He stops before my door, steps forward, knocks, steps back. Stands still. He waits. I don't know. His clothes are nice.

The bags were by the door. I had yet to take them out. I was going to take them out. I had said that I would take the bags out and I was going to do it. I was waiting until it was dark. When it got dark I would take them out. That was my plan.

There is not enough. There should be more. This is what they say to me. This is what they tell me. No matter what, they always tell me they want more. I tell them, fine. I say, okay. I'll get you more, I tell them.

I got them ready. I lined them up along the wall and got them ready. I put the smallest ones in front, the biggest ones in back. The in-between ones I put in between. Then I took a picture. I have not regretted it.

The floor was clean. I had cleaned it. Same with the sink. I had cleaned it too.

I come home and change my clothes. I put on a pair of shorts, a t-shirt. I open all the windows. I turn on the fan. I sit down in a chair. Lean forward. Close my eyes. I should fill a jar with water. Put it in the fridge.

They were in their bed together. It was late. They were tired. She was talking.

"When you were a child," she said, "did you say your prayers before you went to bed?"

He was on his stomach.

"Now I lay me down to sleep, the Lord I pray my soul to keep. Like that," she said. "That kind of thing."

He propped himself up on his elbows.

"No," he said.

"Me either," she said.

He reached out a hand and placed it on her leg. She looked at him and then got out of bed. She got on her knees by the side of the bed and folded her hands in front of her face.

"You don't even have any clothes on," he said.

"Shh," she said.

He watched her close her eyes. He could see her lips moving.

I lock the door and turn around. The man is there. On my front lawn. I take a step toward him, then stop. I nod my head. Say hello. The man moves his lips. I ask if there is something wrong. Is there something I can do for him? Is there something that he wants from me? The man stands still. He stands still and stares. I nod my head. I turn around, unlock the door. I go inside.

He may come today. He told me he would come today. I'm not going to wait here, though. If I am here and he comes, fine. But I'm not going to wait.

My wife and I sleep on the floor. On a mattress on the floor. We sleep on two of them. Two single mattresses. Pushed together. Tight.

There were no lights on, no lights that I could see, but I went up anyway. I knocked. I knocked twice. No one answered. I knocked again. I rang the doorbell. I waited. Nothing happened. No one came.

All of us were there. We were there. They were there. They were late, but they were there. They had something with them. They held it out. We looked at it. We reached for it.

She tugged at it and then he pulled it out.
"You broke it," she said.
He tried putting it back in.
"It's broken," she said.
He tried to put it back.
"Don't move," he said.
He set it into place.
"Stay there."

They keep getting shorter. They keep getting shorter and shorter. They keep getting shorter and shorter and shorter.

They had sex and then she left. When he got up he read the note. Then he taped it to the wall beside the other notes. He made breakfast.

It wasn't moving. I was on top of it, pushing. It wouldn't break. It had been broken before. But I didn't break it. I couldn't break it.

I was so close.

I couldn't sleep. I drank a glass of milk and then made breakfast, careful not to wake my wife.

There were three of them. They were in a room together. They were in a room together waiting.

"How much longer?" one said.

The other two were silent.

"It won't be long now," one said.

The other two were silent.

I want something that has never happened before to happen now.

Now.

I went with him. He wanted me to go with him. He wanted someone to go with him. I was there with him. I said that I would go with him. We went. We were there.

He was late again. The next time is the last time, he was told the last time.

He was not afraid.

This time was the last time, though. He was told to leave. As soon as he sat down, he was told to leave. He sat still and waited. Everybody waited.

Get up now and go, he was told.

He got up to leave. He stood up to go.

I tell myself I'm ready. I straighten up, breathe slowly. I bend my knees and brace myself. This should not be happening, I know. My mouth comes open. I raise my arms. I know what will happen next. I take another breath.

Listen. Look. This is how it is. This is how it has to be. It really is this simple. This is how it is and this is how it's going to be.

I keep thinking everyone can see it. Everyone can. But I keep thinking everyone will want to see it. That's what I keep thinking. I mean, my God! Just look at it. Just look! Would you not want to see it?

Is it going to happen? I suppose it's possible. It is always possible. I was told that it would happen. So far it has not.

They offered me money. The procedure was simple. They held out their hands. There was money in their hands. "It's yours if you want it," they said. "No one will know," they said. I thought about that. No one would know. How would anyone know? I looked at their list. The instructions were there. I got down on my knees.

He felt his face. He used both hands. Touched the forehead. Pressed the eyelids. He pushed on them. He rubbed his lips. He used his thumbs. His mouth was dry. He bared his teeth. Touched his tongue. He pulled it out.

I got up to go. Went back to bed. I couldn't sleep.

He walks over to where she is and says something. She looks up, sets down her pencil. She stands. Walks away. He follows. She turns a corner, opens a door, steps into a room. Later they emerge together. He shakes her hand and nods. She goes back to where she was. Picks up her pencil.

She touched me. She did. She reached right out and touched me. She touched me when I wasn't looking. I knew that she would touch me. I knew it.

He knew she could do it. He took her to the place. Closed the door. Drew the blinds. He promised not to tell.

It was perfect. I was perfect. I had done it. They all knew it. They all looked. I knew they would. I watched them look. I let them look. I didn't care.

"Are you sick?"

She was on the sofa with a cloth across her forehead. I had just arrived. I had knocked and when she didn't answer I went inside.

"Do you want some water? Or an aspirin?"

I watched her shake her head.

"I could turn the fan on."

"Go away," she said.

I made some soup, brought it to her. She was on the sofa. She was asleep. I took the soup back to the kitchen.

"Where are you going?" she said. She was sitting up. The cloth was off her forehead.

"I have to go," I said.

"I feel better now," she said.
"I have to go."

She walks around. I see her out there sometimes, walking. Now and then she stops. She stares. Then she starts to walk again.

He looked at his watch. He unfastened it and took it off. Put it in his pocket. He put his arm down at his side. He held it there. He did not move.

There was no one there. There was no one who had seen him.

He was not afraid.

I went back. I said I wouldn't. But I did. There was no one there. No one saw me there. I went back and looked.

I came home, took off my clothes. I washed my hands. Checked for stains. I ran a bath. I brushed my teeth. I brushed them twice. Got into bed. I tried to sleep.

He was glad to see me. I was glad to see him. I let him do what he does best. Then I made him dinner. I undressed and went to bed. He was there beside me. I could hear him breathe.

Have I mentioned money yet? I don't think I've mentioned money yet. Maybe I should do that now. What about it? Would you like to know? Would you like to know where I get my money? Or do you only want to know how much?

What should I say? Should I say this? Or should I say that? Either way, I want this to end. I want it to be over. I'd like to start again. But I need to stop. I have to stop before I can start again. I have to make this stop.

This is all true. All of this is true.

I was on the sofa. I was sitting on the sofa. My wife was at the table. She was playing solitaire. I was on the sofa, reading. It was Sunday evening. We were drinking wine. The radio was on.

I no longer want them. I don't want any of them. Do you know someone who wants them? Tell them they can have them. They can have them all. I do not want any. You must know someone. There must be someone somewhere. Someone somewhere must want these.

I admit. I look at it. Sometimes I look at it. I can't believe it's mine. Other times I wonder why. I wonder why I bother. I probably shouldn't bother.

I was afraid. No, I wasn't. I wasn't afraid. I thought I was. I thought I would be. But I wasn't. I wasn't afraid.

It doesn't have to be big. In fact, it isn't going to be big. It will actually be quite small. Or should I say slim? Slim might be more appropriate. Because it will be slim. It already is slim. It was always slim. Even before it existed, it was slim.

They found it finally. It took them longer than I thought, but finally they found it. I went over there to look. It was sticking up. Half of it was sticking up. I reached out to touch it, then did not. There were men with masks and gloves. Two men held a bag. They will need another bag, I thought. They bent it, though, and then it fit. I looked at the hole it left. You could hardly even tell.

There was something wrong. Something wasn't right. That was obvious. I pretended not to notice. If he did something wrong or something that I thought unnatural, I said nothing. In fact, I imitated him. Not imitated, really. Emulated. I began to think there was something wrong with me. I asked him if he noticed anything, if he thought I had changed in any way. But he didn't know what I meant.

They killed him swiftly and with ease. It was getting rid of him that was difficult. They had thought to bury him, but did not wish to dig a grave. Neither did they wish to risk discovery depositing the body in the river. They resorted to dismemberment. They had wanted to avoid dismemberment, but in the end they resorted to dismemberment.

They cut him into cubes.

I tried to make myself clear. No one understood me. I said it again. No one knew what I was saying. I spoke quietly and clearly. I took my time. Still, no one understood. I told them one last time. I waited until they were sleeping and then I told them once and for all.

I will get up.
I will have a bath.
I will get ready.
I will go to work.

I held the bowl and watched him fill it. I could barely stand the sight of it. I would empty it, bring it back. Then he would fill it up again. He had filled it twice already. He bent over it and moaned. Nothing came out. I let him wait, then try again. I took the bowl and left the room.

I do what I do. Even on days when I don't, I do.

What if I get caught? What then? It's not too late to stop. I'll stop. I'll say I changed my mind. I can change my mind, can't I?

I get paid today.

My job was to keep the watch. To keep the watch is not the best of jobs. There are better jobs. The patrol, for example. But that position was not offered me. The watch was what was offered me. I took the watch. I kept the watch. The watch was mine to keep.

She wanted him to show it to her. He didn't want her to see it, though. "You promised," she said. He had promised. She promised not to touch it. He told her he would show her if she promised him she would.

Let them look. Go ahead. Let them look. It doesn't matter. Honestly. They don't know.

Do you think they know? They don't. Believe me. They don't know.

He tried to lift it. He had to move it. He knew he had to move it. He pushed it. He braced himself. But it would not move. He could not move it. He yelled for help.

The gift was in a box. The box was on the table. I had yet to open the box. I was going to wrap it first.

I put it here myself. I think I put it here. I know I wrote it down. I remember doing that. Maybe on my desk. My desk is such a mess. But where else would it be? I went through my wallet. It isn't in my wallet. It has to be right here. It must be somewhere here.

It was big. I had never seen one so big. I couldn't believe it. But there it was. In front of me. It was massive. Huge. It was up to me to move it. I would have to make it move. I would have to touch it. I could not believe it. It was never going to move. I was never going to make it move. I put on my gloves.

I did it again. I said I wouldn't, but I did. I did it with both hands. I had the TV going. I won't do it again, though. I don't regret a thing.

I haven't shown it to anybody. Not so far, at least. So far, no one else has seen it.

Listen to me. I am telling you. Listen. I will not say anything. I promise, I won't. No matter what happens, I will not say anything. But nothing will happen. Trust me. Nothing will happen. No one will know. No one will know until it's too late. Then we'll be gone. We will be gone, won't we?

It was their mistake.

There was one there. I took it out. It was not the only one. Other ones were there.

It was spotless. I made sure. I washed it thoroughly. I let it dry. Then I did it once again. I wiped it off and looked at it.

I was almost pleased. After going over it. I went over it and I was almost pleased.

I finished it. I just sat down and finished it. I started it and finished it. I did not get up.

Think about it. All I'm asking you to do is think about it. Just think about it.

I'll have another drink, I thought. I'll have another drink and then I'll go to bed. Then it will be time for bed.

I want it to be over. Finished. Done.

I slow down. I speak slower.

I have enough to do it now. I could do it now. I might do it now.

I think this might be it. I really do, I think it might be. I might finally be done. I feel as though I'm done. I feel as though I'm finished, actually. I don't think that I can do much more. I can't do any more.

I want to go home. I always do. No matter where I am or what I'm doing. I just want to go home.

They killed him after dark. Night had its advantages. So they waited until dark. There were two of them who killed. It took the two of them to kill. The two of them took turns. First one of them killed. Then the other.

The killing happened quickly. It was over quickly. The body lay unmoving. The killers stood above it. Then they knelt beside it. They picked up the body. Put it in a bag. They took the bag outside. Then they went back in. They went back in and wiped the floor. The body they disposed of. The body and the bag.

He wondered what it was. He tried removing it, but it would not come off. He made calls. Inquiries. Produced explanations. Constructed theories. Every morning there was more of it. It grew bigger and got darker. Until it covered the carpet. Changed the color of the carpet. Became, in fact, the carpet. At which point he'd forgotten it.

It came off. I pulled it off. I peeled it off. It was off and in my hand. I was holding onto it. I held it up and looked at it. It looked like nothing I had ever seen before. I tried to put it on again. I thought that I should put it on again. But I could not. It would not go on. It was off and it would not go on.

Okay, that's it, forget it. I changed my mind. I don't want to talk about it. No, no, no, no, no. Forget it. I changed my mind. Just forget about it. Please.

I watched him break them. He did it slowly. His face had no expression. He did not make any noise. I was shocked. Surely it felt good. It must have felt good. I asked him if I could break one. But he wouldn't let me. Not this time, he said. I watched him break another. Some of them he crushed. I thought he might save one for me. There were not many left. He had the last one in his hand. He broke that one then too.

They were there. They were all there. They had been there for a while. Waiting. They were waiting there. They said that they were waiting. I did not believe them. I did not. They left. When I arrived, they left. They all got up and left. So maybe it was true.

I was there too long. I was there for far too long. I should not have stayed so long. I should have left before I did. I should have got up and gone home.

They tell me to tell them. They tell me to tell them everything. Not to leave out anything. But I do not remember more. I've told them everything I know. But that is not enough. They tell me they want more.

I reached in and found it. I grabbed. I pulled. But it didn't come out. So I let go and grabbed it again. I grabbed it harder this time–took good hold and pulled. But it did not come out. It gave a little, though. I reached in with both hands.

He gathered up his things and put them in a box. He put the box beside the door, took off his tie. He put his tie into the box. He sat down at his desk. He put his feet up on his desk. He leaned back in his chair. The phone began to ring. It stopped. He looked at his watch. He took off his watch and put it in the box.

How many of them should there be? Should there be more? Will there always be more? What if one day there aren't any more? What if one day that is it?

We decided not to use them all. We decided we could not. We did, of course, use some of them. Some of them we had to use. But we did not use all of them. We did not come close to using all of them.

I am not done. I am nowhere near to being done. I have so much more to do. I thought I might be done. I thought I almost might be done. But I am not.

That's it. That's everything. It's almost everything. There may be other things. Smaller things. Shorter things. Snippets of things.

He cut it into cubes. He did it carefully. He took his time. He put the cubes on a tray. He put the tray in the freezer. Froze them individually. When they were frozen he packaged them. He put the packages in the freezer, used them when he needed them.

No one has to know.
No one ever will.

What do you think? You've had time to look. Tell me what you think. Be honest. Tell the truth. Not that it will matter.

Everyone was gone. Everyone was already gone. I was not yet gone. But I was going.

"Do you want to stay?"

"I do," I said.

But I didn't.

I got what I wanted. I got a lot of it. They sent some of it the first time. Then they sent some more of it. But they never sent all of it.

It is hot and I am drinking coffee. When I say hot, I mean it's hot. Too hot to be drinking coffee.

This afternoon I watched basketball. My wife worked crossword puzzles at the table. Sometimes she looked up.

"New York wins," I said.

"Good," she said.

I did not get up to get it. I was ready to. I was going to get it. But I did not.

I don't know.

I thought I might get up to get it.

It was midnight. It was almost midnight. He was still awake. He had not yet been to bed. He was in the kitchen. He was eating toast. His wife was in the room. She was dressed for bed. She had been in bed. He offered her some toast. She smiled and shook her head. She kissed him on the cheek. Said goodnight and left the room. He watched her walk away. He looked toward the clock. He took a bite of toast.

I was afraid to finish. I was afraid. I finished. I was left alone. I didn't know what would happen. I had nowhere that I had to go. I had nothing that I had to do.

I spoke when I was spoken to. I kept my mouth shut otherwise.

Did I misrepresent myself? No. I did not. I did use another name. But I did not misrepresent myself.

I used my own address.

I used my own number, too.

I was cold. My hands were cold. I had on gloves. But my hands were cold. I clenched my fists. My arms still shook. I hugged myself.

I still have them. Some of them. Some of them I kept. I couldn't throw them all away. Not at that time I could not. I could do it now, I guess. I go through them now and then and wonder.

I spent the morning cleaning. I dusted. I swept. I got down on my knees. I cleaned beneath the bed. I mopped the bathroom floor. I scrubbed the bathtub. Scrubbed the sink. I thought the walls could use some paint. I opened all the windows, both the doors. A breeze blew through. That was better. That felt better. I was ready.

As the undisputed kings of underground publishing, Sam Hiyate and his Gutter Press go where few dare – offering the best contemporary writing by authors such as Bruce LaBruce, Karen Connelly, Derek McCormack, Golda Fried, James R. Wallen, Christine Slater, John L'Ecuyer, Barbra Leslie, Tamas Dobozy, Nathalie Stephens, N.J. Dodic, Struan Sinclair, Guy Babineau, Donna Lypchuk, Danny Vinik, and Scott Symons.

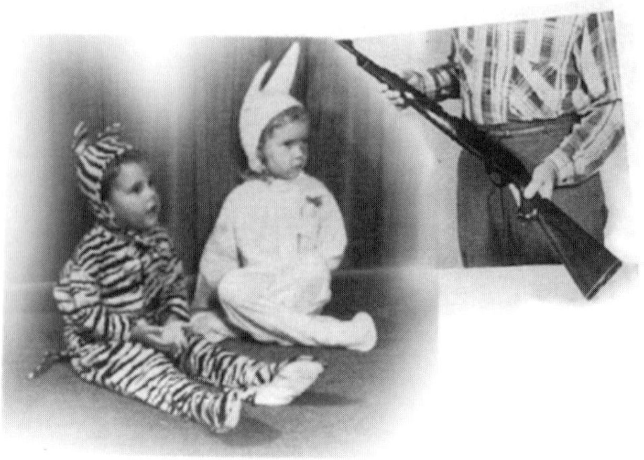

For more information on our titles, visit *www.gutterpress.com.*